When her father was kidnapped, Olivia Flaversham asked Basil the great mouse detective for his help.

But no one knew just how dangerous it was going to be. The evil master criminal Professor Ratigan was behind the plot...

Designed by Howard Matthews and Chris Reed, using stills from the film.

British Library Cataloguing in Publication Data

Walt Disney's Basil the great mouse
    detective.—(Disney stories).
    I. Walt Disney Productions
    823'.914[J]   PZ7
    ISBN 0-7214-1033-2

First edition

WALT DISNEY

BASIL
the Great Mouse Detective

Ladybird Books

It was a great day for everyone in Mousedom. Queen Mousetoria was celebrating sixty glorious years on the throne, and there were to be tea parties followed by fireworks and dancing in the streets.

But Mr Flaversham the toymaker couldn't afford to take the day off. He had too much work to do. As he bustled about his workshop, his daughter Olivia played happily with the wonderful dancing doll her father had made for her birthday.

Suddenly, a great shadow fell across the window. It frightened Olivia so much that she hid in a cupboard. When at last she peeped out, a vicious-looking  bat with a wooden leg had burst into the room. She watched helplessly as the bat tied up her father and dragged him from the house.

What was she to do?

Olivia ran outside, but her father was nowhere to be seen. Through the streets she trudged, asking everyone she met for news of a peg-legged bat carrying off an elderly mouse. But no one had heard or seen a thing.

At last Olivia crept inside an old boot. Tired and downhearted, she began to weep. She loved her father very much.

Her sobs were heard by Dr David Q Dawson, a portly gentlemouse who couldn't bear to see a damsel in distress. He gave Olivia his handkerchief, and after one last sniffle Olivia told him her story.

As he listened, Dr Dawson stroked his mouse-tache. He was worried. There could be no doubt about it. Olivia Flaversham's father had been bat-napped.

Olivia had read about a famous detective known as Basil of Baker Street. She asked her new friend to take her to see him, and at last he agreed.

They were shown into the great mouse's presence by Mrs Judson, the motherly housekeeper, and Olivia once more told her tale.

As she described the peg-legged bat, Basil's eyes began to gleam. 'Aha!' he exclaimed. 'I know him

well. His name is Fidget and he works for my
arch-enemy, Professor Ratigan. I've been trying to
capture that twisted genius for years.'

So Basil of Baker Street, the great mouse
detective, agreed to help Olivia Flaversham. He
intended to put a stop once and for all to the evil
doings of Professor Ratigan.

Meanwhile, the evil professor was lurking in his secret den amid the sewers of London. He was stroking Felicia, his monstrous pet cat, who purred delightedly as the professor patted her over-dimpled chops.

'I've decided to become King of Mousedom,' the professor announced to the ruffians who worked for him, and they all gave three loyal cheers at the news.

10

'This evening, Queen Mousetoria will tell her subjects that she has chosen me as their King.'

The ruffians gasped, wondering how Ratigan would get her to say that.

'I intend to capture the real Queen,' went on the professor, 'and substitute a mechanical doll that will say exactly what I want it to say.'

The ruffians gasped again. This was Professor Ratigan's master plan! It was a stroke of pure evil. The man was a genius!

As the professor spoke, Fidget brought in the old toymaker, Olivia's father, and Professor Ratigan had him locked up in a workshop.

'Now, Fidget,' said the professor, 'Flaversham is going to make my mechanical Queen, but it's possible that he will object. So I have a little scheme to make him change his mind!'

Professor Ratigan then gave Fidget a list of some things he wanted him to fetch. One of them was Olivia Flaversham!

Slowly, Fidget read through the list. His little bat-lips moved as he read the difficult words. *Get...the...following...tools...gears...girl... uniforms.*

Fidget sniggered. This was the sort of job he liked. But he did wonder what a *following* was, and where you got it.

Now Professor Ratigan guessed that Olivia would consult Basil of Baker Street, so he instructed the one-legged bat to go first to the great detective's house and stamp about under the window.

It was Olivia who spotted the strange marks outside. *Footstep and peg...footstep and peg... footstep and peg.*

'They must be Fidget's tracks!' she cried. 'He's been spying on us.'

'After him!' yelled Dr Dawson.

'Wait!' said Basil. 'This is a job for my faithful Toby.'

He gave a curious whistle, and into the room trotted a mighty bloodhound. His nose was quivering with excitement at the work that lay ahead.

Basil, the doctor and Olivia all climbed on to Toby's back and set off through the cobbled streets. Fidget's scent was so revolting that the bloodhound had no difficulty in following it.

To their surprise, it led to a toyshop.

Inside the toyshop, Basil made an alarming discovery. The mechanical parts of several dolls had been removed. Also missing were the uniforms belonging to the toy soldiers.

Basil stood lost in thought, working out what it all meant. Suddenly there was a blood curdling screech. Using his wooden leg as a pole, Fidget vaulted out of his hiding place inside a doll's cradle. He dragged Olivia onto a high shelf and stuffed her into the sack he was carrying.

But as Fidget escaped with his booty through a window in the roof, Professor Ratigan's list fluttered

down to the floor. It landed at the feet of
Basil of Baker Street.

The great detective
had got his first real
clue!

As soon as Fidget got back to Ratigan's den, the evil professor went in to see Flaversham.

'Now then!' he snarled. 'Here are the spare parts you need, and here is your daughter. If you don't finish making a mechanical Queen by 8 o'clock tonight, I shall feed Olivia to my beautiful Felicia.'

The bloated Felicia sat up, her purple ribbon twitching at her master's words. She loved snacks between meals. She'd had nothing to eat for a good ten minutes, and she was famished.

So Mr Flaversham set to work as hard as he could. Whatever the cost, he was determined to prevent Olivia from ending up as the cat's supper.

Meanwhile, Basil had returned to Baker Street where he performed some scientific tests on Fidget's list. Then he murmured, 'Ratigan's hide-out is somewhere near the port of London.'

'How do you deduce that?' asked Dr Dawson in amazement.

'Elementary, my dear Dawson,' replied the great detective. 'There are traces of seawater and whisky on this paper. Where will you find *both* these substances? In a tavern used by seafarers, I think.'

So Basil and Dr Dawson, disguised as sailors, searched the inns of dockland. At last, in the seediest one of all they caught a glimpse of the peg-legged bat disappearing through a hole in the wall.

They gave chase. Little did they think that they were rushing headlong into a villainous trap set by Professor Ratigan, the Napoleon of crime.

The trail of the peg-legged bat led Basil and Dr
Dawson through a maze of pipes to a trap door.
Cautiously they pushed it open, to find themselves
in a dingy cellar. On the floor was a bottle, and
corked up inside it was Olivia Flaversham!

As they set about releasing her, the cellar
suddenly was flooded with light. Surrounding
them was a gang of toughs.

'It was a trap!' groaned Basil. 'What a fool I've
been!'

'How true!' purred a silky voice from the
doorway. 'How very true!'

There stood Ratigan.

'Tie them up!' he hissed, and the toughs sprang to do his bidding. 'Now!' he continued, 'Let me tell you about the horrible fate I've planned for you both.'

And Ratigan's voice quivered with pleasure as he spoke.

Basil and Dr Dawson were tied side by side to a mousetrap. Pointing at them was a cross-bow, fitted with a deadly arrow. A gun, too, was aimed at them, and a sharp axe hung overhead.

'This is what will happen,' said the professor. 'When that phonograph finishes playing, the string tied to its needle arm will tip over that sherry glass.' Here the professor pointed upwards. 'A steel marble will fall out of the sherry glass and roll down that chute.' Here the professor pointed out the chute. 'When it reaches the bottom, the marble will hit the catch of your mousetrap, and the trap will spring.'

In case they had missed the point, Ratigan explained that the spring would cut off their heads.

'But just in case it doesn't,' he went on remorselessly, 'the axe will fall, the cross-bow will fire, and the gun will go off.'

And with a mocking laugh, Ratigan set off with his crew for the palace, leaving Basil and Dr Dawson to face their hideous fate alone.

Basil of Baker Street was depressed. It seemed that Ratigan had won, after all. But Dr Dawson still had faith in Basil's brilliant brain.

'Think!' he urged. 'You must get us out of this mess! Mousedom depends on you!'

And Basil had a sudden brainwave. If he and Dr Dawson could waggle their feet at the crucial moment, they could make the mousetrap move! If so, the marble would miss the catch, and the trap wouldn't spring!

On the other hand, he thought gloomily, *the arrow from the cross-bow, or the bullet from the gun, not to mention the axe hanging overhead, might get us with a lucky hit.*

The record on the phonograph was scratching towards its close. The moment of truth had arrived.

'Prepare to waggle!' Basil commanded. So, as the fatal marble slid along the chute, Basil and Dr Dawson waggled for all they were worth. The trap inched backwards, and the marble missed the catch. They were not to be beheaded after all!

They flinched as the axe fell, but it passed between them and cut through the cords that

bound them to the trap. The bullet and the arrow whistled harmlessly past their heads.

With one bound, Basil was on his feet. 'Come on, Dawson!' he cried. 'We must save our beloved Queen Mousetoria!'

Basil pulled from his pocket a special dog-whistle and blew soundlessly upon it. Back in Baker Street, Toby pricked up his ears and stretched. *Time to sort out Felicia,* he thought, rising to his feet.

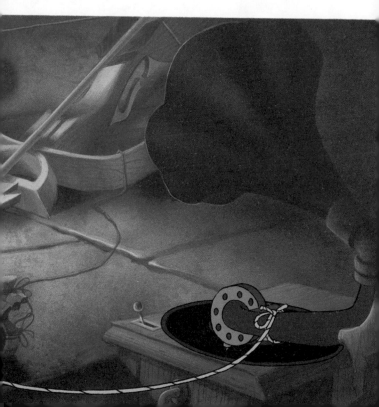

Basil and Dr Dawson arrived at the palace just in time to save Queen Mousetoria from being hurled off a balcony by Fidget, who was now disguised as a one-legged Beefeater.

The monstrous Felicia was waiting below to receive the royal titbit. She was feeling peckish again.

Fidget fled in terror from Basil and the good doctor, who immediately hurried towards the great hall where the mechanical Queen was already making her speech.

But Toby stayed behind. He gave a joyful *woof!* and chased the corpulent cat towards the Palace watch-dogs. Within minutes came the sound of slavering and a licking of lips. But of Felicia there was no sign.

Only a bedraggled purple ribbon was left to tell the tale.

At that very moment, the mechanical Queen announced that she intended to marry the wonderful Professor Ratigan. All the mice were struck dumb at the news, and they shuddered as Ratigan made his entrance, already dressed in royal robes.

'I am your King!' he proclaimed. 'I declare that slavery is restored, and taxes are doubled.'

'Imposter!' screamed Queen Mousetoria.

'What did you say?' Ratigan gasped in astonishment.

'Imposter!' repeated the Queen. Suddenly she went into a fast spin, and bits of her started to drop off. Right in front of her astonished subjects, Queen Mousetoria appeared to fall to pieces.

Basil had taken over the controls!

Ratigan stared open mouthed at the wreckage of Flaversham's doll. He knew that his master plan had failed.

Then Basil stepped forward and told the subjects of Queen Mousetoria that the professor was nothing but a foul *stentus rodentus:* in other words, a sewer rat!

At this point, Ratigan screamed with rage, and dashed towards a balcony.

Grabbing Olivia as a hostage, he jumped onto his airship which was tethered outside. Fidget was already aboard, and the villains made their escape together.

But Basil wasn't
finished yet! Snatching
up some bunches of
festive balloons, and
the red white and blue
flag of Mousedom, he
constructed an airship
of his own, and set off
in pursuit.

Through the skies
above London went Ratigan, with Basil and his
friends not far behind. Basil was definitely gaining,
when there came a great cry of 'Look out!'

Ratigan had crashed into Big Ben! So it was that
the two sworn enemies, Basil of Baker Street and

Professor Ratigan, the evil genius of crime, fought their last battle amid the secret workings of London's great clock. It was time for the showdown.

Basil managed to work his airship close to Big Ben, and jumped on to the clock. Then he snatched Olivia from the villain's foul clutches and passed her safely into the waiting arms of

Mr Flaversham and the doctor. But, as he did so, Ratigan dealt him a mighty blow from behind.

Basil fell from the parapet towards the ground below.

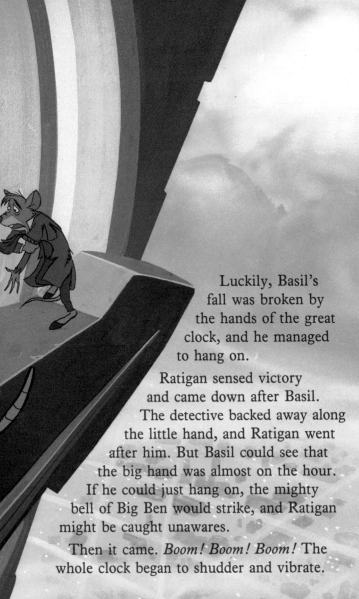

Luckily, Basil's
fall was broken by
the hands of the great
clock, and he managed
to hang on.

Ratigan sensed victory
and came down after Basil.
The detective backed away along
the little hand, and Ratigan went
after him. But Basil could see that
the big hand was almost on the hour.
If he could just hang on, the mighty
bell of Big Ben would strike, and Ratigan
might be caught unawares.

Then it came. *Boom! Boom! Boom!* The
whole clock began to shudder and vibrate.

Basil lost his grip on the little hand, but as he fell he managed to catch hold of Ratigan's airship. Ratigan tumbled after him, and saved himself by clutching onto Basil's cloak.

The two enemies struggled wildly in mid air. Their weight was too great for the ropes that held the propeller to the airship, and suddenly they snapped.

With a scream of rage, Ratigan pitched towards the ground far, far below. For one moment Basil hung there. Then, still gripping the propeller, he too began to plummet down.

In the little airship, Olivia burst into wild sobbing. As her father and Dr Dawson tried to comfort her, they all heard a whirring and creaking noise. Looking down in astonishment they saw a propeller heading up towards them! And there was Basil, riding it like a bicycle!

Willing hands soon pulled him aboard. Basil the great mouse detective had triumphed yet again!

The evening editions of all the newspapers
carried an account of Basil's sensational adventures.
They announced that Queen Mousetoria would
present him with a special medal.

Back in Baker Street, Olivia hugged the great
detective and thanked him for his help. Then she

and her father returned home to the toys they'd left behind them.

But Dr Dawson stayed on, and was ever afterwards introduced to Basil's clients as 'my trusted associate'. The two friends worked together on many cases, but none was sweeter to Dawson than the case of the mechanical Queen – his very first adventure with Basil, the great mouse detective of Baker Street.